D1207257

The Golden Bough

A Fairytale Ballet For Children

Written and Illustrated by Wilor Bluege

Blue Rose Productions
St. Paul, Minnesota

Copyright 1996, 2000
by Wilor Bluege.

All rights reserved. No part of this book may be staged theatrically, videographically, or cinematically, reproduced or transmitted in any form or by any means, electronic or mechanical, including photocopying, recording, or by any information storage and retrieval system, without permission in writing from the author.

ISBN 1-883477-39-5
Library of Congress CIP 99-068849
Printed in Canada

Lone Oak Press
Red Wing, Minnesota 55066.

To all my wonderful students.
W.B.

Once upon a time, a tree stood in a clearing in the middle of a wood at the edge of a village. The tree had a golden bough, and on the bough was a golden cage, and in the cage was a golden bird. The people from the village didn't know how it happened to be there, and they didn't know why. It had just always been that way, although stories had been rumored about a wizard and an evil spell that had been cast on the bird.

Whatever the truth behind the mystery of the golden bough and the burden it carried, the little golden bird had been sitting in that golden cage for as long as anyone could remember. It never sang, although it opened its mouth mutely as if it wanted to, and its golden feathers drooped disconsolately. It was such a sad sight that no one ever wanted to go there (besides, they were afraid of the evil spell), so the little bird was very lonely and sad.

Somehow, everyone had come to believe that if anyone ever let the golden bird out of the cage, an enormous hole would open up in the ground, and that person would be swallowed up immediately by the earth — and not just that person, but the whole village and all its people as well! There would be no evidence that a village had been there at all! People just went on about their lives and were reasonably happy. They danced in the village square and tried to forget about the little golden bird in its golden cage.

The little bird never sang, and its golden feathers drooped disconsolately.

Things had gone on like this forever, but then one day, after the dancing was over, a little girl wandered into the woods. She had always felt very sad for the little bird. Perhaps because she was lonely herself she could feel the misery of the little bird more keenly than anyone else. When she went to the clearing, there was the tree with the golden bough and the golden cage with its small, golden-feathered inhabitant. She was so affected by the sight of the little bird that she couldn't help what she did next.

Without thinking, she opened the cage! The little bird flew out faster than you can blink your eyes and fluttered about in the trees of the wood. The little girl called out to the little bird, "Oh, please come back! Please don't be afraid!"

It was only then that she remembered the curse. She closed

her eyes, gritted her teeth and waited for the earth to open up and swallow her on the spot. But nothing happened. She opened first one eye and then the other. Still nothing happened. What could this mean? Could all the stories have been lies?

The only thing that *did* happen is that suddenly all the birds of the wood were chirruping, singing and carrying on as if it were spring even though spring was three months away! High up in the branches flew the little golden bird. As it flew off, it looked back over its shoulder at the little girl and said, "Because you released me from my golden cage, I will be your friend forever, and whenever you need me, I will come to you."

Time passed . . .

The little bird flew from its cage faster than you can blink your eyes.

The little girl didn't tell anyone about what she had done, or that the little bird was out of its cage, because that would have panicked the people in the village. She knew no one ever went into the wood, so no one would ever know her secret. She continued to go to the clearing in the wood, hoping to catch a glimpse of her friend, but the golden cage still hung empty, with its door open.

One day on her way through the woods, it started to snow. First a single snowflake, then another, and another began to fall. Soon snow was swirling all around her and piling up in drifts. Leaping through the drifts, she hurried to the clearing, fearing that perhaps the little bird might have gotten caught in the snowstorm.

Her heart sank, for there, on the bottom of the cage, was the little golden bird. It had tried to come back to the safety of the tree, but the cold and snow had nearly frozen it. Yet the little girl would not give up. Gently she picked up the lifeless form of the little bird. She held it in her hands and breathed softly on the little bird to warm it. She held it close to her heart and began to sing to it while she danced. Then, something miraculous began to occur: The snow began to melt away. As she stroked the little bird, she

felt a slight fluttering of the little bird's heart next to her own. Then, the little bird gave a shudder and shook its wings. "You're alive! You're alive!" the little girl exclaimed.

"Thank you!" said the little bird. They were so happy that they danced all around the clearing together. And everywhere they set foot, flowers sprang up out of the ground. They were not very quiet about it either! Each flower had something to say to the others. "My dear, aren't you looking fine today!" said the Wood Sorrel to the Nodding Trillium. The blue Gentians were all talking at once, and the Jack-in-the-Pulpit was very preachy, going

Even the little Pipsissewa, who was normally very shy could scarcely contain her excitement.

The Willows were particularly lovely in their light golden gowns.

on as usual about the state of the woods. Even the little Pipsissewa, who was normally very shy and kept to herself in the woods, could scarcely contain her excitement. "It's spring! It's spring!" she piped, and began dancing all around the meadow.

The yellow Cowslips were engaged in their annual discussion over their proper name. One insisted on being called a Cowslip, while another argued, "How can you say you're a Cowslip, when your mother was a Marsh Marigold?" Another said, "I'm not one to be nitpicky about such things," (which wasn't true, because everybody knew he was *always* nitpicky about such things), "but I believe the proper name is *Caltha palustris*. And, if I'm not mistaken, I seem to recall that your own father was from a highly respected family, the Buttercups of Foggy Bottom." The discussion went on like that for quite some time.

Then the tree spirits, the dryads, got into the act. The Willows were particularly lovely in their light golden gowns. The Oaks and Maples came with their red- and

yellow-tasseled flowers. A stately, dark green Conifer moved with dignified grace. Though there were still small epaulets of snow on her shoulders, all her fingertips sported the latest fashion in soft, light green nail polish. All together, it was a most festive — not to mention noisy — display.

The Conifer danced with the Columbines, and the Cowslips finally stopped arguing long enough to bow to the Gentians when they asked them to dance. Soon all the flowers and dryads were dancing, with the little girl and the golden bird right smack in the middle of everything.

The ruckus attracted the children from the village, who peeped out between the trees to see

what the celebration was all about. Before long, everyone was dancing a Maypole dance and having a grand time. The golden bird and the little girl danced until long after everyone else got tired and went home; they danced until even the flowers were nodding their heads sleepily. Finally however, the little bird said, "It's time for you to go home now. Your parents will be worried. Don't be sad. Because you released me from my cage and saved me from the snowstorm, I will come to you whenever you need me." Then, with a flick of its tail, a cock of its head, and a wink of its eye, the little bird flew off.

The Cowslips finally stopped arguing long enough to bow to the Gentians when they asked them to dance.

Time passed . . .

The Conifer danced with the Columbines.

The little girl had not seen the little golden bird for a long while. She wondered how her little friend was, but she was in school and had lots of homework, so she could not get to the clearing in the woods for several months.

Walking home from school one day past the edge of the woods, she suddenly heard cries of distress coming from the woods. She rushed to the clearing in time to see the little golden bird struggling against ropes that some horrible, wicked creatures had thrown around it. The little bird was pinned to the ground, almost exhausted, and the awful creatures were nearly upon it.

Now, the little girl was very shrewd, for she knew that you cannot overcome such things with physical violence. There was only one thing that was effective: She pulled out some blank paper from

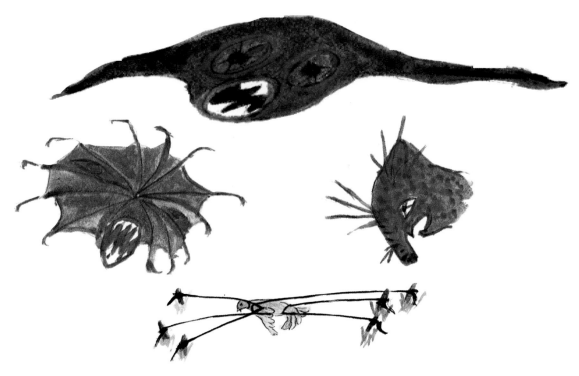

The little bird was pinned to the ground, almost exhausted, and the awful creatures were nearly upon it.

her school notebook and began writing furiously on one sheet of paper after another. On each she wrote the name of one of the horrible creatures. She knew that names are magic, and that if you know the name of something you have power to overcome it. The little girl ran from one monster to the next, placing a name on each one. One was called "Fear," . . . another, "Self-Doubt," . . . another, "Envy," . . . another, "Hatred." On and on she raced, and every time she placed a name on one of the demons, it dissolved into a pile of ashes that the wind then swept away with its broom.

However, no sooner had the little girl completed this than another monster, more hideous than all the rest, oozed out of the woods. It was a trickster and changed shapes so quickly and frequently that the little girl was at a loss to know its name. She'd had experience with all the other demons before, so she knew their names, but this one was more powerful than all the rest combined. The little girl cast about in her mind for a name, but she had used up all the names she could think of! What could she do?

The awful blob was almost on top of the exhausted little bird, who had now lost consciousness. If the little girl did not do something very quickly, the little bird would be suffocated. With a flash of insight, the little girl suddenly remembered that she had a small mirror in her school bag. She grabbed the mirror and ran between the demon and the little bird. She held the mirror out in front of her, so that the demon could see itself in the mirror.

When the demon saw itself, it shrieked in horror as if it had been mortally wounded and began slowly shrinking and backing away. The little girl stood her ground until the monster had dwindled to nothing and finally slipped away back into the woods, a mere puddle of its former self. Finally, she made one more sign, "The Unknown," and put it on a stake at the edge of the wood, so that the demon-without-a-name would know that it could never come any further than that ever again. She knew it would always be there, but, she reasoned, The Unknown might just as easily be unimaginably wonderful as unimaginably horrible, so one did not have to be unduly afraid of it.

The little girl ran to her friend, quickly took out the pocket knife from her school bag and cut through the ropes that held the little bird down. She picked the little bird up and helped it to move its wings again, which had been so cruelly bound by the ropes. Fortunately, nothing had been broken, and the little bird once again expressed its undying gratitude to the little girl and promised to come to her aid if she ever needed help. The little bird flew off once again.

Time passed . . .

The little girl was on her way to her first day in a new school. She was feeling lonely and scared, because she didn't know anybody in the new school, or who her teacher would be. Suddenly, the little golden bird appeared. It sat on her shoulder and said, "Because you released me from my cage, and saved me from the snowstorm and the demon monsters, I will be your companion and go with you to your new school."

"But they don't allow birds in school," the little girl said despondently.

"I will make myself invisible," chirped the little bird. "No one will be able to see or hear me but you." So the little girl went to school, and the little golden bird sometimes sat quietly on her shoulder and sometimes fluttered up to the top of the blackboard where it seemed to take great interest in what the teacher was writing. The antics of the little

The little golden bird sometimes fluttered up to the top of the blackboard, where it seemed to take great interest in what the teacher was writing.

bird fluttering about the teacher and the room brought a smile to the little girl's face and made her feel so much better. After school, the little girl was walking home. The little bird said, "I must go now, but I will return, whenever you need me." The little bird flew off towards the woods.

The next day, a group of bullies stopped the little girl on her way to school. They taunted her and treated her meanly. The little girl couldn't bear to go to school, so she ran to the clearing in the woods and sat on a rock, crying as if her heart would break. Suddenly, the little bird appeared. "Because you released me from my cage, and saved me from the snowstorm and the demon monsters, I will give you the gift of a joyous heart that no one can take away from you." Then the little bird began to do a silly little dance that made the little girl laugh. The little bird swooped down and brushed the little girl's feet with one of its golden wings and said, "Now take off your old shoes." By magic, the little girl's feet were now snugly fitted into the most wonderful, magical shoes she had ever seen.

The little bird taught the little girl how to dance in those wonderful shoes, and when they were done, the little girl felt like she could face the bullies. With her new magic shoes on her feet, she started back to school again.

When the bullies showed up, the little girl tossed her head, stood up for herself in her new pointe shoes, and left the bullies with their mouths hanging open in amazement as she danced off to school.

It wasn't long before the next dilemma occurred. She saw another girl cheating on a test at school. She knew that cheating is wrong, but she didn't want to be a tattletale either. After all, she was the new girl in

The little bird taught the little girl how to dance in those wonderful shoes.

school, and she wanted to make friends, not make the other children dislike her. The little girl went to the woods to think about what to do. The little bird appeared and sat quietly on her shoulder for a moment, assessing the situation, which somehow it already seemed to understand.

Finally, it whispered into the little girl's ear, "Because you released me from my cage, and saved me from the snowstorm and the demon monsters, I will give you the gift of wisdom."

Suddenly, it became clear to the little girl how she could handle the situation. She went to the other girl and said, "Would you help me with my homework? I think it would help me a lot, and it might help you, too, if we could study together. It would be fun!" So the two studied together underneath the tree with the golden bough everyday, while the little golden bird flew above them in the tree tops.

Studying was difficult at first. The small letters didn't seem to know if they were coming or going, and so the "d" kept being mistaken for a "b." The "g" kept flipping its tail to the wrong side, becoming a "q" instead. Generally speaking, the letters did not seem capable of organizing themselves in the proper order, particularly when the "i's" and "e's" got together. The "i" completely lost its head and ran madly after it as it rolled away.

For their part, the numbers simply would not fall into place and kept arguing about who was the most important. The "1" thought it was more important than the "9" — to which the nine took great offense. The whole thing became so chaotic that the letters and numbers finally landed in a jumbled heap.

The two little girls shook their heads in dismay at the tangled mass of numbers and dangling participles. A firm hand was obviously needed. "Now see here," they said, pulling at the tangled heap. "You simply *must* do better! We will have no more arguing or fighting. You will conduct yourselves in an orderly and disciplined manner from now on." After that, things went more smoothly, and all the letters and numbers cooperated nicely.

Then, one day, the little girl's friend said, "I have a confession to make. I used to be afraid that I wasn't smart enough to get good

All the letters and numbers landed in a jumbled heap.

grades, so sometimes I cheated on tests. But now I know that I'm not stupid, and that I can learn just as well as anybody else. I think we are both going to do very well on our next test." And so it was. Both little girls aced the next test — without cheating! Best of all, the girls became best friends!

Time passed . . .

School was out for the summer, and the little girl was feeling very lonely because her best friend had gone away with her parents on a vacation, and she didn't have anybody to play with. She went to the clearing in the woods and lay down in the warm grass in the meadow. The little bird appeared and assessed the situation immediately. As it flew off quickly again, it chirruped gaily, "Because you released me from my cage, and saved me from the snowstorm and the demon monsters, I will give you the gift of friends." Before long the little bird came back, leading a parade of little girls.

Everyone began to dance, and soon the whole village was there, dancing and having the most marvelous picnic. As evening came, the dryads came out with their little fairy lanterns. The little girl looked around her and saw all the wonderful friends she had made that day. Knowing that there would be many

Before long the little bird came back leading, a parade of little girls.

more beautiful days to come (it was summer, after all), she didn't feel sad as she waved goodnight to her friends.

As the moon rose above the trees and bathed the tall grass in silver light, the little girl noticed the tree with the golden bough. It had been standing on that spot for so many years, but something had changed. Now the *whole* tree, not just the one branch, was glistening gold, and there was something written on the bough where the empty cage still hung. The little girl approached the tree and ran her fingers slowly over the letters . . .

while the little golden bird danced joyously in the moonlight.

THE END

Costume Sketches for the Ballet

The Little Girl

The Golden Bird

The Dryads

Oak Dryad   *Willow Dryad*   *Conifer Dryad*   *Maple Dryad*

Costume Sketches for the Ballet

Nodding Trillium

Pipsissewa

Columbine

Jacqueline-in-the-Pulpit

Cowslip

Gentian

Wood Sorrel

Flower Spirits

Costume Sketches for the Ballet

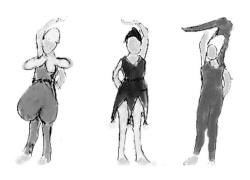

Wood Sorrel, Columbine, Jack-in-the-Pulpit

Gentian, Cowslip, Pipsissewa, Nodding Trillium

Flowers

Pink Flower Girl

Yellow Flower Girls

Flower Girls

Costume Sketches for the Ballet

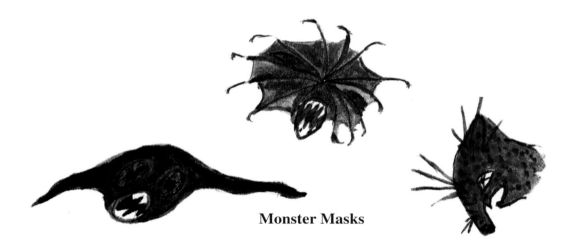

Monster Masks

Friends

Bullies

School Girls

Costume Sketches for the Ballet

Winds

Time Passers

Villager

Best Friend

Snows

Costume Sketches for the Ballet

Letters and Numbers (front and back views)

About the author . . .

Wilor Bluege is a teacher and choreographer of classical ballet and character dance, working in St. Paul, Minnesota. She traces her balletic roots through the Russian branch of classical ballet and the Ballet Russe. As a performer, she danced soloist and principle roles in *Swan Lake, Sleeping Beauty, Giselle, Les Sylphides, Pas de Quatre, Nutcracker, Vivaldi Concerto,* and *Scheherazade*; and excerpted principle roles from *Legend of Love* and *Don Quixote.*

She has choreographed many works, including the full-length ballet production of *"The Golden Bough"* which premiered in St. Paul in November of 1997 and continues to enchant audiences annually with its beautifully painted sets, rich costuming, and choreography.

Wilor has a B.A. in biology and psychology from St. Olaf College. She is a lecturer as well as a teacher and has created several presentations weaving together her passion for dance with a variety of other interests. Titles include: *The Bag Lady Wore Toe Shoes, Archetypal Themes in the Classical Ballet, Dance and the Task of Becoming Human, And A Wolf Shall Devour The Sun, Spirituality and the Environment, Art and the Soul.*